HANNAH MONTANA
THE MOVIE

GOING HOME

Adapted by Lara Bergen
Based on the screenplay written by Dan Berendsen
Based on characters created by Michael Poryes and Rich Correll & Barry O'Brien
Executive Producers Michael Poryes and Steve Peterman, David Blocker
Produced by Alfred Gough and Miles Millar
Directed by Peter Chelsom

DISNEY PRESS

New York

Printed in the United States of America

First Edition

1 3 5 7 9 10 8 6 4 2

Library of Congress Catalog Card Number: 2008910427

ISBN 978-1-4231-1820-6

For more Disney Press fun, visit www.disneybooks.com

Visit www.disney.com/HannahMontanaMovie

Chapter 1

Miley Stewart was no ordinary girl. She got to be a normal teenager. She was also secretly Hannah Montana, the world's biggest pop star. It was the best of both worlds.

Lately Hannah's concert tour had kept Miley very busy. She was so busy she couldn't even help her best friend, Lilly, plan her Sweet Sixteen party.

Now the tour was over. Miley was glad that she would get to go to Lilly's party. Lilly was glad, too!

Lilly was also a little nervous. The party was that afternoon, and there were still so many things to do. She really needed Miley's help.

"As soon as the bell rings, we've got to bolt," Lilly told Miley.

"I'm totally there," Miley said.

Then Hannah's publicist, Vita, showed up with some big, *big* news.

Vita told Miley that Hannah had been asked to sing at an award show in New York.

"What am I going to sing? What am I going to wear?" asked Miley.

Vita already had a car out front. "Hannah has got to do a major shop!" she said.

What about my party? Lilly wondered as she watched Miley go.

"Minor Hannah emergency," Miley explained. "I'll be there. Promise."

Chapter 2

Shopping as Hannah took much longer than Miley expected. Miley couldn't believe how different it was. Photographers followed her everywhere. Plus, all the stores wanted to give her clothes for free!

"You're a star," Vita told her.

Miley had so much fun shopping as Hannah that she lost track of the time. Then she suddenly remembered Lilly's party. She was late!

Reporters were still following Hannah. If Miley got out of the limo as her real self, they would figure out her secret.

Miley finally decided that she had no choice. She would have to go to Lilly's party as Hannah.

At the party, everyone was excited to see Hannah. No one paid any attention to Lilly.

"I swear I'll make it up to you," Miley told her friend.

"You will never, ever, *ever* be able to make it up to me," Lilly said.

Chapter 3

Miley had more problems at home. She had forgotten about going to Tennessee for her grandma Ruby's birthday.

Miley wanted to go to New York. Her dad didn't agree.

Finally, Miley and her family flew away.

When Miley got off the plane, they
were in Tennessee. Miley's dad knew how
much she loved to sing. Hannah Montana
had let her do that and still have a normal
life. But now Hannah was starting to
become *too* important.

Mr. Stewart told his daughter that for the next two weeks, she had to stay Miley. He wanted to see if she still knew how to be herself.

"You can't take Hannah away from me," Miley told him.

"Really?" he said. "'Cause that's what I'm doing."

Chapter 4

It had been a long time since Miley had been back in her hometown of Crowley Corners, Tennessee. She didn't even recognize her old horse, Blue Jeans. Or her old friend, Travis. Everyone remembered her, though.

Travis was working on Grandma Ruby's farm for the summer. "I rebuild the chicken coop," he explained to Miley, "and I get to sell the eggs."

"So that's really all you want to do?" Miley asked him.

"You just don't get this place, do you?" Travis said.

Travis tried to show Miley what she
had been missing. He led her on a ride on
Blue Jeans. He even took Miley back to
the watering hole where they had played
in first grade.

"Look, there's jumpy rock," said Miley.
"And our swing!"

From then on, Miley and Travis met at the watering hole each day. Miley also helped Travis fix up the chicken coop. Thanks to him, she was starting to feel at home in Tennessee again. Then she found out something that made her upset.

Chapter 5

Developers were trying to buy up the prettiest part of Crowley Corners and turn it into a giant shopping mall. If the town didn't raise enough money to pay the taxes on the land, the developers would get it. Time was running out.

Then Travis had a great idea. Miley had told him that she knew Hannah Montana.

"Maybe she could give a benefit concert!" Travis said.

"I guess I could give her a call . . ." Miley said.

Her dad had said no Hannah for two weeks. But he told her this would be okay—the concert was for a good cause. Of course, he wasn't sure how Hannah was going to get to Crowley Corners. Luckily, Miley had a plan.

A few days later, a car pulled up in front of Grandma Ruby's.

Vita stepped out along with Lilly, who was dressed up as Hannah.

"Thank you! Thank you! Thank you!" Miley told Lilly. She was so happy her friend had forgiven her. "I swear, Hannah will never come between us again."

Chapter 6

Miley was so excited. She really liked Travis, and he had asked her out to dinner. Of course, she had said yes. Then she found out that *Hannah* had to have dinner with the mayor that very same evening. Lilly thought Miley should cancel with Travis.

Miley knew that Hannah couldn't back out of the mayor's dinner. She didn't want to cancel on Travis, either. She thought she could do both.

Her plan worked . . . but only for a little while. In the end, it was a disaster! She wasn't at either dinner for long.

Then Travis caught Miley dressed half as herself and half as Hannah.

"Have you been lying to me this whole time?" Travis asked her. "Just forget it, Miley . . . Hannah . . . whoever you are. We're done."

Chapter 7

Trying to be both Hannah and Miley had backfired on Miley—again.

She was sure that Travis would never forgive her. But she still wanted to make it up to him. So Miley worked all night long and finished fixing up the chicken coop.

By the time Travis saw the coop, Miley was singing as Hannah in the center of town. Travis followed the sounds of the cheering crowd until he saw her.

When Miley saw Travis, she couldn't go on.

"I've loved being a star, but I don't think I can do it anymore. At least not here," she told the audience. "This is home. . . . This is family. And there are only so many sacrifices you can ask a family to make. The last time I stood on this stage, I was six. I was just Miley. I still am."

Then Miley took off her wig. She had remembered that her home and family were more important than being a star.

"Thanks for letting me live my Hannah," she said.

To Miley's surprise, her family, friends, and fans weren't ready to let Hannah go.

"Please be Hannah!" they called out. "We'll keep your secret!"

"It's too late," Miley told them. "I can't."

"Sure you can!" Travis said.

"Hannah's part of you," said Lilly. "Don't let her go."

So Miley put the wig back on and sang another one of Hannah's songs.

In the end, Hannah kept Crowley Corners from changing forever. And Miley kept herself from changing too much, as well.

She had the best of both worlds . . . again!